To Jude, for your inspiration, and to my little Amelia – D.H.
To Leo, with love – J.D.

First published in Great Britain in 2008 by
Frances Lincoln Children's Books, 4 Torriano Mews,
Torriano Avenue, London NW5 2RZ
www.franceslincoln.com

British Library Cataloguing in Publication Data
available on request

ISBN 978-1-84507-644-3

Illustrated with acrylics

Set in Berkeley

Printed in China
1 3 5 7 9 8 6 4 2

The Faraway Island

Dianne Hofmeyr

Illustrated by Jude Daly

F
FRANCES LINCOLN
CHILDREN'S BOOKS

There once was an unhappy
man who longed to be all
on his own. He had spent his
life sailing the seas and no
longer felt at home with
anybody. He was so unhappy
that he growled and snarled
at people like a monster.

"Give me a boat," he said
to his captain. "Then I can
row to an island."

But the captain refused.
So the man jumped off the
side of the ship and swam to
a barren rock that stuck up
out of the rolling sea, further
away from anywhere than
anywhere else in the world.

And there he was – alone as can be, while the wind howled
and the ocean roared and his ship disappeared over the horizon.
After some time, he crawled to a cave, made a seaweed nest
for himself, and slept.

The next morning, at the edge
of the hissing waves, the man
found a bag of rice washed
overboard from the ship
and a half-drowned cockerel.
He coaxed some life into the
cockerel, fed it a few grains
of rice and planted the rest.
Then he found fresh water
to drink and mussels to eat.

So the man went on living on the barren piece of rock. And he would have gone on like this, but one day the sky turned dark, the sea leapt high and the wind blew a ship towards his island.

When the sailors came ashore, the man ran into his cave.

"Go away!" he growled into his beard.

The sailors stood in front of the cave. "Oi! Anybody there?" they called.

Silence.

So they gathered the rice that seemed to grow wild, and when the ocean stopped heaving and hissing, they left behind a lemon tree – just in case – and went back to their ship.

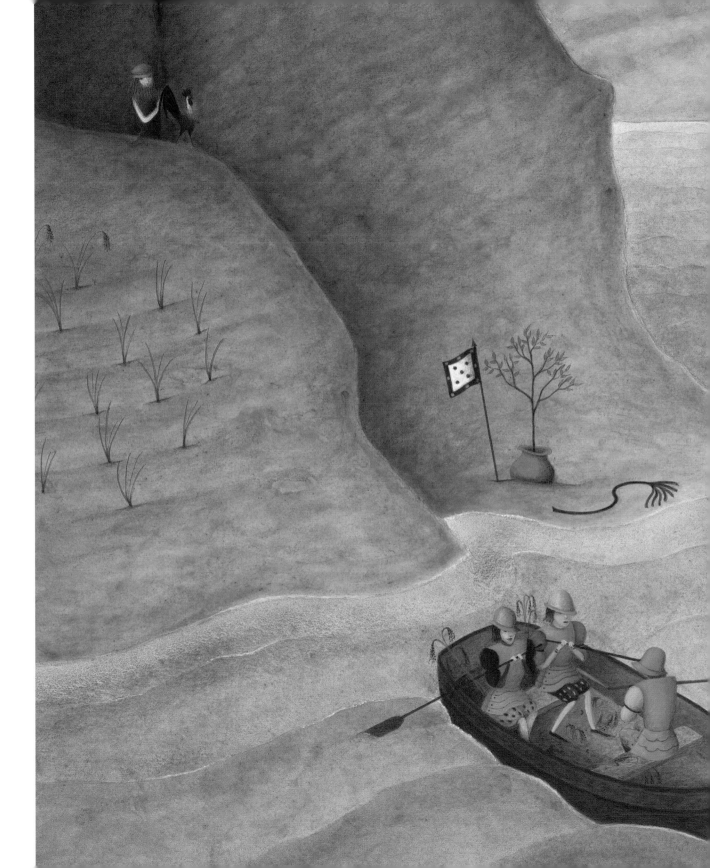

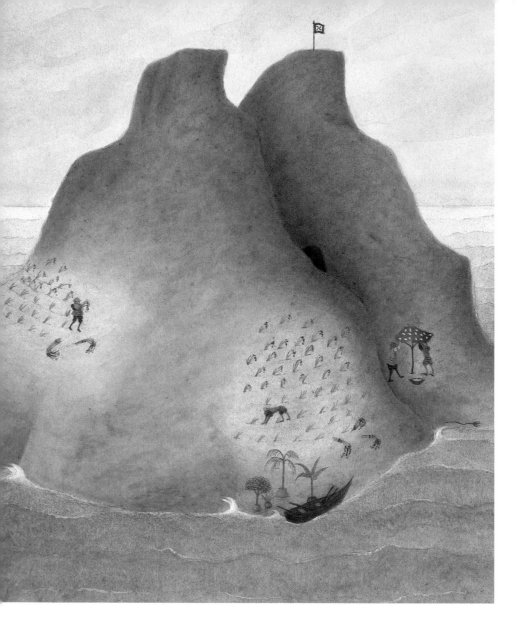

After some time another ship was blown ashore. The sailors gathered rice and lemons and left behind a banana tree, a pineapple plant, a pomegranate tree and a date palm – just in case.

When next they came to the island, they found fat bananas, juicy pineapples and pomegranates and plump dates growing there, and when they saw them, their mouths watered. They peered into the cave.

"Oi! Anybody there?" Silence.

"Oi! Is this your garden?" Silence.

So they picked… and picked some more.

"Oi! How can we repay you?" Silence.

So they left behind hens, ducks, goats, peacocks, guinea-fowl and some snuffling pigs – just in case.

In time, the Queen of Portugal heard of the miraculous island where sailors had planted her flag, and how it had changed from a barren rock into a rich garden. She sent a messenger to the island.

Outside the cave, the messenger coughed politely, then said, "The Queen summons you."

Inside, the man breathed hard. He shook his head. "I cannot go!"

"The Queen demands it!" said the messenger. "And queens have to be obeyed!"

So one dark, moonless night, the messenger rowed the unhappy man out to the Queen's ship.

"Keep away!" the man hissed from behind his beard, as he scurried below deck.

When he arrived at the palace, the Queen declared, "You have fed my sailors on your faraway island. As a reward, anything you desire shall be yours."

The man peered out from behind his beard. "There is nothing I wish for, Your Majesty."

"Nothing? Not even a castle?"

He shook his head. "I have a cave."

"A ship, perhaps?"

"I don't wish to travel."

"A kingdom?" asked the Queen.

"I have an island."

"Then what do you need?"

"All I need is to be left alone. Don't you see…?"

"See what?" said the Queen.

"I'm a monster!"

The Queen stepped forward. She pushed the man's hair aside
and looked into his face. She took his hands and examined them.

   She shook her head. "I don't see a monster."

   "What do you see?"

   "I see a gardener."

The man looked out at the glittering, crowded city
and thought of his island sticking up out of the rolling sea.
Suddenly he was in a rush to leave.

Just then, the Queen's seamstress stopped her stitching and glanced up. She caught a mysterious gleam in the man's eyes: the gleam of a faraway place – and something else. And at that very moment, she decided there was more to life than mending the Queen's underwear.

So she followed him out through the castle gate.
"Go back!" the man hissed over his shoulder.

"Leave me alone!" he growled, as he hurried through the city.

"Keep away!" he snarled, as he scurried below the ship's deck.

But the seamstress took no notice. And on the long
journey she busied herself mending the ship's sails.

When the man stepped ashore on his far distant island, there she was again, following right behind him.

"What are you doing here?" he demanded.

But the seamstress just hummed and set to work planting the seeds she had brought with her.

So the days passed in silence as they worked, digging and planting,
until their hands were rough and their lips tasted of salt. Plants took
root, flowers blossomed, creepers twined and curled, trees grew tall,
forests formed, and birds flocked to roost on the island that was
no longer barren rock.

Then the man looked up into the dark leafiness of his island. Something else had started to grow. Even the air had changed. Something was twining and growing and taking root deep inside him.

Suddenly he knew what it was.

"I'm not a monster!

I never was!"

He spread his arms wide in the green light, threw back his head and laughed. He had found what he was searching for.

HAPPINESS!

About the story

Fernando Lopez arrived in Goa in 1510 to claim land for the Portuguese Empire. Under the leadership of General D'Alboquerque the fortress was captured, but due to a lack of military strength D'Alboquerque returned to Portugal to fetch more soldiers and warships, leaving Lopez in charge.

On his return, he believed Lopez had become too friendly with the local people and punished him by torture and disfigurement. Lopez went into hiding and later took passage on a ship bound for Portugal. When the ship stopped at the deserted island of St Helena to take on fresh water, he no longer felt able to face his wife and children, and jumped ship.

A year later, the crew of a passing ship were amazed to find signs of a bed and Portuguese clothes in a cave, but couldn't find the man himself. As more ships began calling, Lopez learnt to be less afraid and in return for fresh provisions, sailors gave him gifts of seeds, plants and livestock. The exotic flora brought from all parts of the world flourished and gave the island the look of a botanical garden. Oak and citrus grew alongside bamboo, banana, pineapple and pomegranate.

This is how the island of St Helena became fixed in people's minds as a rich garden growing on a rock in a distant ocean… with a man ruling over it like a king